THE ARTISTRY OF MAGIC

Helen De Cruz

Pink Hydra Press

2025

Copyright

The Artistry of Magic
© Helen De Cruz 2025

Cover art by Helen De Cruz

Paperback: 978-0-6398430-4-9
e-book: 978-0-6398430-5-6

Pink Hydra Press
www.thepinkhydra.com

"In this love story between a homeless magician and a scholar of ancient books De Cruz brings to life an Oxford that is as once as real as a slap and as sweetly lyrical as a childhood dream. Her world is a world of class divides and chalk drawings that come to life: poignant, beautiful, romantic, and wry. Maarten and Johanna are characters you will take into your heart and treasure. And who will teach you things you always knew but somehow never saw as clearly – about art and love. And magic."

—Eric Kaplan, television writer and producer (Big Bang Theory, Futurama)

Acknowledgments

This story grew slowly over the years. It incorporates my experience living in Amsterdam, Oxford, and Ghent. The city of Haltra has elements of all these marvelous cities. The novella benefitted from the helpful comments of several people: Eric L. Kaplan, Sharon Shinn, Fiona Moore, Steven French, Aliénor De Smedt. Thank you so much for your insights! I am very indebted to Johan De Smedt for sharing his experiences of life on the streets (which he did for two years), as it allowed me insight into a very marginalized identity and difficult way of life.

MAARTEN

MAARTEN DIDN'T SMELL TODAY. When you live on the streets, smells tend to seek you out and cling to you, no matter how clean you try to keep yourself. He had just found a set of men's clothes on a trash heap: an almost-white shirt, a vest with faded embroidery that still had all the buttons on, a short woolen jacket, and breeches without holes. All his size, though too roomy.

With the confidence that fresh clothes afford, he began his work for the day. He boldly approached the entrance to the Library of the College of Liberal Arts. He stared up at its high stained-glass windows, imagining how resplendent they would look from inside. Yet even here, outside, he could feel the magical force emanate from the vast collection of ancient books. Exactly what he needed. He knelt on the pavement to start his work.

As mist still hung in the narrow streets of Haltra that early spring morning, Maarten took the drawing chalks out of his tattered bag and looked around for inspiration. On the dewy cobblestones, a dead sparrow lay, wings folded, intact beak slightly opened within its partially decomposed head. Maarten reckoned it starved. Well, *he* wouldn't.

Visualizing the creature in better surroundings, he drew a mysterious forest with birds poking their heads out of the golden foliage. A small group began to gather around him as he drew, and they cried out in delight and wonder as the chalk-outlined birds hopped from one branch to another. The work had a high level of detail, further heightened by the magical animation. A robin opened its beak, and its thin voice filled the cool morning air around the now-hushed crowd. Maarten watched with satisfaction as stuivers, and even a few gulden, landed on the notice that read, *Help feed a hungry magician*.

Maarten sat next to his work, allowing the admiration

of the growing crowd to flow inside him and lift him up. He didn't think of his work as begging, or even as busking, but as *art*—art accessible to everyone, gratuities optional. He had just turned thirty, but he looked older, weathered as he was by years of life on the streets. He was tall and had deep-set dark eyes in a thin pale face, eyes that critically gauged his chalk art and scanned his surroundings.

A middle-aged, short, fat woman with a mass of red curly hair stepped forward from the back of the crowd, her black Scholar's robes pulled tight around her. She cleared her throat and said in a low, husky voice, "Sir? I am sorry, but I have to ask you to leave. You cannot draw in front of the library."

The audience dissipated quickly. The fat woman continued, apologetic, "I hate to do this, but you're upsetting the magical balance of the library."

As if, Maarten thought. *They're probably so understaffed nobody even knows where half the books are, let alone the effects of the proximity of magicians.* But many years and more beatings than he cared to remember had taught Maarten it was unwise to protest. He got up and began to gather his chalks. The librarian, as he assumed she must be, asked him to erase the work. He sighed, pulled an old dirty rag out of his bag, and wiped the floor. The magical forest became a blurry mess.

TWO DAYS LATER, Maarten went up to the Quarter That Studies again. The city of Haltra was divided into four Quarters of unequal size and wealth. To the north lay the Quarter That Studies and the Quarter That Prays. To the south, the Quarter That Trades and the Quarter That Works, the largest and most populous parts of the city. At the city's heart was the Center That Rules with the City Council and Magistrate's buildings, their spindly towers visible from all the Quarters. Many winding canals crossed through these quarters, with colorful snakes of narrow-boats moored hull to stern.

Maarten could draw unmolested in the Quarter That Works where he and his two friends had set up their camp, and even in some parts of the Quarter That Trades, in the sleazy neighborhoods with their opium dens, liquor booths, and whorehouses. Why, then, was he drawn to the Quarter That Studies? It was for the glory, he concluded. He loved the opulent glass windows and carved stone walls of the scholarly buildings of Haltra. That sense of glory was worth the occasional beating.

For now, while his clothes still appeared clean (though no longer smelled clean), he could risk it. As he colored in the outlines of his new chalk drawing, he saw that librarian again. There was that familiar dodge maneuver he'd seen so many times: the way she cast down her glance to avoid eye contact, the way she circumvented his work to reach the staff entrance. That awkward dance she did to avoid acknowledging his humanity, even in a brief moment, in a nod, a meeting of eyes. That was the way he was always made invisible. There was nothing subtle about it, but then, rules of etiquette did not apply between streetfolk and housed people.

But today, he would have none of it.

Ignoring that she ignored him, he said, his voice flat in the cool morning air, "I'm not drawing on the books' force, as you see my pictures ain't moving."

"That's an exquisite drawing!" the librarian mumbled. "That must be the Prophetess Blanceflor?"

Maarten said smoothly, with the no-hard-feelings smile that he had cultivated over the years: "You're right, it's her. I see madam is an expert in the arts." The Prophetess drove her own chariot, a halo around her head, whip in her right hand, her eyes ablaze with the terrifying second sight.

The woman said, "Look, I'm sorry I had to chase you away yesterday. Everyone who works here has to swear an oath to not allow any magic to be performed in the library or its surroundings, and that's what you were doing. But let me make it up to you. I'll buy you some food."

"No thank you," Maarten replied coolly. "If you like my art, gratuities are appreciated, but I don't need no food handouts."

Looking up, he saw a cleaning crew approach, a large, closed carriage drawn by black horses, with Haltra's blazon on its side, two red carps circling each other. As he deliberated whether to make a run for it, a thin old man leapt out the carriage with the surprising suppleness of a predator.

"Are we alright here?" he asked, glancing at the woman's Scholar's robes.

She said, nodding to Maarten, "I'm fine. He's with me."

The crew moved on, the horses' hoofbeats and clanging of wheels on the cobblestones growing fainter, but another one could be heard approaching. She said, "Let's go into Carla's coffeehouse, over there."

THEY FOUND SEATS at one of the narrow tables. Long, age-yellowed mirrors lined the back wall, interspersed with portraits of grave-looking men and women in black robes and starched collars. Maarten glanced around uneasily, resisting the urge to wolf down his first decent meal in weeks, a small meat pie. He cautiously sniffed, then tried, his first cup of coffee. It turned out to be a foul-tasting liquid he could not imagine people might fork out so much cash for. The librarian dug into her small tartine with gusto.

They made brief introductions. Maarten said as little as

politeness allowed about himself, offering only his first name, and that he had come to Haltra to make street art. This was his way with strangers. There was little privacy to be had on the streets, but his memories, his identity—they were his own. The librarian's name was Johanna de Vries—a pretty name, Maarten thought.

He said, "So you're a Scholar."

Johanna beamed at him, blue eyes flashing with pride. "I'm only a Librarian—bottom of the pecking order, and all that. Still, it took me seventeen years to get here! From the Quarter That Trades to the Quarter That Studies, from my mother's little greengrocer's shop to *this*." She gestured around at the grand paintings of scholars and the stained-glass roses on the windows that looked out onto the street. "And you, it seems, are a Magician?"

"Am I? I ain't got the robes, or any fancy silver rings, neither." Maarten stated the obvious, but it was an open question: Is one a Magician by virtue of one's innate ability and practiced skills, or by one's social station? He was inclined to think the latter.

"But you possess the gift of magic! I do not wish to pry

. . . but why are you begging in the streets? Magicians are so rare nowadays. You could be an officer on a war campaign, or a civil servant in the Quarter That Rules, or you could use your skill to fashion intricate handiwork in the Quarter That Trades."

Maarten patiently explained to her that the objects he needed for his craft were hard to come by. Old books or jewelry or other rare precious objects were housed in libraries and in the homes of wealthy civilians. "So, it is not that we've become rarer in terms of innate ability—just that it's harder to get the tools we need," he concluded.

Johanna leaned on both elbows as she sipped her coffee, fascinated.

"It's a force like gravity. Like with the books." He gestured toward the street.

"How about now?" she asked. "Are we too far away from the library for you to . . . channel it?"

"Focus it and amplify it. Let me try." He fixed his eyes on the table. The little silver spoon hovered briefly over his cup, then plunged into the black bitter brew. "It ain't spectacular, sorry."

Nevertheless, Johanna was enchanted. He recognized that look on her face: mouth somewhat agape, round, shining eyes, raised eyebrows. The look of wonderment. Magic, he often thought, was foremost in the mind of the beholder. He could have performed any conjurer's trick and she'd treat it as the greatest feat of sorcery. But he felt pleased at a woman wondering at him—that had not happened for a long time.

JOHANNA

EVERY WEEKDAY, JOHANNA WALKED to the Library from her narrowboat, which lay moored on the Broadlei, the canal that ran in an east-west direction between the Quarter That Studies and the Quarter That Trades.

When she woke up, mist still clung in thin shrouds to the water's surface, dampening the din of the belfry's carillon from the Center That Rules, which stood visible across the water. Her feet nimbly negotiated the bobbing floor of the single large space that made up the boat's interior. She fed her cat, Sammie, who began each day with a crescendo of increasingly insistent meows. Over the years, he had carefully calibrated this morning routine, as she would throw various things at him, not all of which he had managed to dodge.

Johanna saw Maarten daily, as he worked far away from the library yet close enough to use faint traces of its magic to create subtle animations in his drawings. He evoked distant worlds through them: Prophetesses riding their chariots with eyes ablaze, pastorals with dancing shepherdesses and grazing sheep, temple domes in tender hues of blue and white in the distance.

Every day, they spoke briefly. The drawings and what they depicted were a natural starting point for conversations. Following an impulse, Johanna invited Maarten for lunch again. He looked up at her with that skeptical look in his deep-set dark eyes, the gaze of someone who has learned to second-guess generosity.

"Not charity," she said quickly, as he began to shake his head. "But as . . . acquaintances?" (Not quite *friends*, she thought.) "What do you say?"

And so she took him to Carla's coffeehouse again. Two other Scholars, Mauritz and Hélène, sat a few tables away in their impeccable black velvet gowns. She could hear Hélène's delicate giggles interspersed with the loud, unrestrained guffaws of Mauritz. Maarten turned around to locate the source of merriment, and said in a gruff voice, "I should go. I'm embarrassing you to your colleagues."

Johanna tried hard not to stare at his increasingly yellow, food-stained shirt. But she said airily, "Oh don't mind them, I am used to it! I'm a Librarian." She lowered her voice. "Whereas those two . . . they're Tutorial Fellows of the College. They don't consider me a proper Scholar."

Johanna had a long history with those two, all the way back to when she'd done the Scholar's exam. All those years she had endured their scorn as she sat studying in the examination halls with the yellow haze of their oil lamps. She sat hunched over heavy books with bleary eyes, as they whispered among themselves, "Poor Johanna, she's from the cheapside. Shopkeeper's daughter! She'll drop out, for sure."

Once the examination halls closed at the stroke of ten of the College bells, they would go home to their handsome *burger* houses with their gables and stained glass windows. Johanna would still have to haul around heavy sacks of flour at her mother's greengrocer's shop, late into the night. Whenever their derision got to her, she would mutter quietly, "You *also* trade, you bunch of *verdomde* hypocrites." She *would* make it. And she did. Unfortunately, her mother did not live to see that day.

Maarten broke her reverie, saying, "I'm sorry about this. I didn't mean to be embarrassing you, but having clean clothes is a real challenge for us streetfolk. The women in the wash house don't let me in, and I obviously can't pay someone for the service."

Johanna asked, indulging in her curiosity, "So how *do* you get clean clothes?"

"Trash heaps," he replied. "Or charity, occasionally. It's far easier than getting them washed."

Johanna could hear the elder Tutorial Fellow, Mauritz, mumble, "And now she's sitting there with an actual tramp." He raised his voice a little. "Hey, Johanna, why don't you introduce us to your boyfriend?" Hélène hid her mouth behind her hand.

Johanna continued to ignore them, but Maarten finally got up, white knuckles of both fists planted on the table. "That's it. I can't pull you into my problems, Johanna."

He turned around and strode off in a dignified manner. Johanna watched him leave, throwing the front door shut behind him. All she could think was, *he called me Johanna.*

THE NEXT MORNING, Maarten gave the briefest of nods to Johanna, then continued with his drawing. It was completely immobile, yet it evoked movement through artful strokes of loose white over dark green: a woman in a long, white lace underskirt leapt high in the air for a dance, a gavotte perhaps, her pointy, elegant shoes darting over the floor.

Johanna picked up her courage and said: "What a beautiful work of art. We can sit outside for lunch today. It is nice out, and all day I am among stuffy books."

As she watched Maarten sitting on the bench, wolfing down a sandwich she had just bought, Johanna considered her motives. Was she happy for the diversion? Was she really interested in him, romantically? Was that even possible, for someone her age, and a Scholar to boot? He was homeless. Nothing could ever happen between them.

Yet, like Maarten, she was a rebel—after all, she lived on a narrowboat. Only people like her and people like him disrupted Haltra's orderliness. Only they crossed the boundaries of the Quarters. She tried to weave points of connection between their vastly different lives, and remarked on how they were similar.

"I see what you're trying to say, but we ain't nothing alike," Maarten said. "Being poor is not some sort of brave act of being unconventional, you know. Unlike me, you can get your clothes washed whenever they get dirty. And they would not assault you and take your shoes away, and drop you off in the middle of the countryside just because they could."

"They would do that?" Johanna asked, trying not to sound incredulous.

"Oh yes, to keep the city clean," Maarten said. "They beat you, then they take your shoes, pull you into one of those black carriages, drive you out into the countryside, and finally, they drop you off, hours away from the city.

You're not technically *banished,* but how to find your way back? By the time you do, your feet are nothing but blisters, all red and swollen . . ."

"I had no idea . . ." Johanna said.

"But that's not all. Next, you've found your way back to your camp where your other stuff is, assuming they didn't throw it away, but you ain't got any shoes. How to find new ones? They don't exactly grow on buildings."

Johanna shifted uncomfortably on the bench, looking at her own practical, slightly worn shoes.

Maarten went on, unrelenting. "You've got no money, you've got no shoes, you'll starve if you can't solve this. It's like this all the time . . . every small thing becomes an insurmountable obstacle. Our lives are very different."

The weather became milder, and so they sat often on benches outside of the library or the scholarly halls. He would tell her about his life on the streets and his magic, his stories of how streetfolk tried to maintain some justice and order among themselves. Like that time when he, Cees, and Jelmer (two fellow buskers and his only friends) went to reclaim Cees's dog, an ugly, adorable mutt that was the envy of everyone and had thus been kidnapped. Maarten had dreaded this confrontation. He didn't like violence, but sometimes it was necessary. Streetfolk had no cleaning crews, which, he added philosophically, was probably for the best.

They had arrived at the thief's camp: big Cees swung around an iron chain, Maarten held a broken glass bottle he hoped he did not have to use, Jelmer was there for moral support. The thief was a very young man who gave the dog back immediately, without a fight. But it died a month later, from unrelated causes.

ONE EARLY SUMMER DAY, when the ancient Halls of Haltra shone in their most delicate yellows, ochres, and browns against a hard blue sky, they sat outside on an elegant iron bench, eating lunch.

"Tell me more about yourself," Maarten asked her. "I'm here talking about myself all the time."

Johanna stared into the middle distance, as if the answer lay somewhere out there. "I live by myself in a narrow-boat. I play the harpsichord and the spinet badly . . . I have a cat." She paused. "And of course, I am a Scholar. I studied theology, though being a Librarian, I don't teach or publish."

Maarten nodded. "That's how you recognized Blance-flor right away."

"I can recite all the noble deeds and radiant words of the Prophetesses," Johanna said.

Maarten glanced at the brick dome of the temple that stood behind them, situated at the edge of the Quarter That Prays. "What do you like about theology?"

"I like the thrill of it, the puzzles," Johanna said. "If a Prophetess can foretell the future, are you truly free in your actions? Imagine, for instance, I had chosen a tartine for lunch, and a Prophetess foretold it. Would I have been able to choose otherwise? And if I hadn't, is my choice truly free?"

Maarten seemed lost in thought for a while. Then he said, "In my mind there's always a natural explanation. Magic can be strange sometimes, but there ain't any gods, or prophetesses who can do anything beyond what we can do. There are also plenty of Magicians who can discern the future with tarot cards or stars."

"There are limits to what magic can do," Johanna said. "See that black stump over there? Many years ago, there was a very large, beautiful plum tree right here. It blossomed in winter and in early spring. The plum tree is the symbol of the persistent Scholar, who often has to work for many years to earn their place through the difficult entrance exams into the Quarter That Studies. Even more so if they don't hail from a family of Scholars. But the tree got damaged one summer by a stroke of lightning, and now there's just a blackened stump. The cleaning crews have not even come around to removing it. If it were revived, that would be a miracle as only a Prophetess would be able to do."

Maarten regarded the stump and said, "I could probably bring that tree back to life. Within each dead plant still lurks a little bit of life force; you only need to find it and coax it out. I can sense it, even now."

"Ah, but why?" Johanna asked. "There is no profit in it. We still need to explain why the Prophetesses work miracles that profit us all. A miracle doesn't necessarily need to violate the laws of nature. A miracle points to the mystery of being. Even a simple act of kindness, at the right moment, can count as a miracle." She put her hand on his arm, as nonchalantly as she could.

"That makes it banal," he objected. "If anything can be a miracle, then nothing is, or *everything* is. Suppose you see a double rainbow? A miracle. My magical chalk drawings? A miracle. The fact that your boat doesn't sink. A miracle . . . No, I've done my share of praying and waiting for miracles, there ain't no such things, any more than there are true Prophetesses."

Maarten

"Maarten, you're so quiet and dreamy lately. Unless I'm mistaken, I discern the signs of love," Cees said, as he, Maarten, and Jelmer sat around a makeshift fire made of rags and dried waste. The evening sun slanted just over an old bridge in the Quarter That Works, where the three friends and traveling companions had set up camp.

Maarten was cooking a simple dinner in a large, dented pot. He had bought the ingredients in a small greengrocer's shop in the cheaper and more shady part of the Quarter That Trades, a shop much like Johanna's mother had had back in the day.

"I swear, Maarten, you're such a masterful cook, I'd eat

shit if you prepared it." Jelmer stared impatiently into the pot as his friend meticulously timed the introduction of each ingredient.

"You're only saying that 'cause I bought the ingredients," Maarten said. The mushrooms had turned light brown and the egg was becoming solid, so he added lentils to the mix.

"You're avoiding the question," Jelmer said. "Cees and I, we're thinking you must be seeing someone."

"Yes, I'm seeing someone," he said evasively, cutting small pieces of parsley into the meal with a rusty pair of scissors.

"This person *does* know it's only temporary, right?—that you'll leave at the end of the summer?" Jelmer probed, as he took out wooden bowls and metal spoons. "We move on, that's what us buskers do. Or are you planning on becoming one of 'em stinking city rats? Is Haltra becoming a tad too comfortable for you?"

In truth, Maarten had become comfortable. He dreaded having to leave Haltra. He felt at home—the buildings, the canals, the people, the little neighborhoods, even

Carla's coffeehouse where he didn't quite fit in. To leave Haltra and go where, exactly? Perhaps to Flanders, or France, or further on, across the channel to Albion? To leave Johanna, to write a note saying, *Sorry, but our worlds are just too far apart. I appreciate our friendship* . . .

"Food's ready!" Maarten said abruptly. He distributed the food into the bowls. His friends dropped the matter. Maarten was grateful for it, and they continued their conversation about unimportant things.

THE DAY CAME THAT JOHANNA invited Maarten into her narrowboat. The boat, painted bright red, lay on the Broad-lei. He could still turn back now. He had no experience with women worth the mention, except for a girl in the village he grew up in, before the accident. The rare women streetfolk usually already had partners. It was somewhat easier for gay men, such as Cees and Jelmer. It did not help that Jelmer had said, with his usual lack of tact and a heavy wink, "You might get lucky today."

He got down the bobbing steps with some difficulty and folded himself into her low, narrow living space. The wooden-paneled concave walls reflected the summer afternoon light. Against one of the walls stood a small spinet. A table with two simple chairs around it was fixed against the wall. He heard a low, rumbling sound coming from under the table.

"Don't pay any attention to that, it's just my cat, Sammie. He's not used to visitors." Maarten saw two angry yellow eyes in a dark face flash at him, ears pulled back.

"Your cat growls, like a dog?" he asked, puzzled.

"He is very protective of this space."

Maarten pointed. "That painting over there, it has some magical amplification."

Johanna took it from the wall. "Really?" She peered at it like she had discovered there was money hidden in the frame. "How can you tell?"

He said, "Don't get too excited, it's only a little bit. Probably not even enough to lift a spoon. How can you see that the Prophetess' dress is pink? You just see it. Similarly, I just *sense* it. Who is this Prophetess? I don't know her."

The Prophetess had a smug smile on her small red mouth. "This is Prophetess Rita. She is very happy in this scene, because she just learned that she can get a chariot and lead the wandering life of a seer, to finally use her gift of foresight. Her husband and eleven children have died of the plague—this happened about a century ago, and it was raging then—and she is delighted, because Nature has finally granted her wish and listened to her earnest entreaties to fulfill her calling."

"Isn't that grand of Nature?" Maarten scoffed. "Killing all those children, so their mother can go off to tell the future."

"We mustn't judge," Johanna objected. "The ways of Nature are unfathomable. We humans do well as long as we are in accord with Nature, and go ill when we work against her."

Maarten had to concede that Nature was indeed inscrutable. Here he was, in the home of a handsome middle-aged woman with likely more experience than him, feeling like a nervous teenager. She hung the painting back on the wall. He gathered his courage and awkwardly tried to wrap his arms around her.

"Tell me if you don't want this," he whispered. Johanna pushed him back on one of the benches fixed to the wall and kissed him with fierce passion.

Johanna

JOHANNA DIDN'T CARE what others thought of her. She never had, or she would not have become a Scholar. She didn't care what other Scholars thought about her and Maarten either. As for the future, who knew? She would play it by ear.

Maarten was working on an ambitious drawing, a military scene with blue-frocked soldiers and rearing white horses. Doublets and stuivers fell into his hat. He cast nervous, frequent glances at it as he continued to work. She stood waiting in the small crowd, until it dispersed.

She cleared her throat and asked, "If you are done, would you like to see the inside of the library?"

"I ain't allowed inside," he said, but he looked eager

nonetheless.

"Leave it to me," she said. "I will vouch for you."

They entered the porter's lodge, and she had Maarten sign the register. He nimbly dipped the pen into the ink-well, and signed simply with "Maarten." She noticed his handwriting was a clean, elegant cursive and wondered at it.

"Now, raise your right hand and repeat after me: I solemnly swear I will not bring any kindle, flame, or magic into the Library."

"I solemnly swear . . ." He looked up at the porter who stood leaning against the double inner doors, looking on with mild interest, and continued: "I won't bring any kindle, flame, or magic into the Library."

They entered the main reading room. Shelves reached all the way to the ceiling. Light fell in through tall, gothic windows, providing an even dusky glow. The floor was tiled black-and-white marble. Heavy books lay open on a wooden table. "So many books, all in one room . . ." he said.

"You haven't seen the best part yet," she said, and guided him into the next room, which was even more splendid than the last.

This was the Fellow's Library, the reading room open exclusively to Tutorial Fellows. The room was airier and more spacious. Worn but handsome Persian rugs decorated the floor. A steady light filtered through a glass cupola above the long central table, providing optimal lighting during the daylight hours for the Fellows as they studied. The two of them were the only people in the room.

She strolled to one of the shelves and picked out a book. It was a theoretical treatise on magic, *De Occulta Philosophica,* by Cornelius Agrippa. Maarten took it, and studied the cover. "I never got to learn Latin. How does a book like this end up here?"

"It is a book on magic." She scrutinized him as he leafed through the book. "It's okay to have this book here, as performing magic isn't allowed in here."

"I know it isn't, the oath and all . . ." he began. "On the other hand, there's nobody else around, and plenty of books to amplify magic from." Maarten got a sly smile.

"Don't do anything . . . rash." She felt nervous. What a terrible mistake to let him into this room. First her favorite café, then her narrowboat, now the library!

He laid the book open on the table, on a double page with drawings of pentacles, astrological signs, and obscure alphabets. He made a small gesture with his right hand. The ink seemed to lift from the page and began to glow. The symbol for the sun (a circle with a dot in it) rose high into the room, halfway to the glass cupola. It transformed into a genuine sun, bright and flashing, and difficult to look at directly. Then, one by one, the Planets lifted out of the page: Mercury rapidly circled around the Sun, Venus and Mars made more relaxed orbits. Out of the planets leapt the gods and goddesses they represented: swift-footed Mercury, Venus with her long, flowing hair, Mars stern and bearded, wearing a helmet.

Johanna gazed at the display, trying to recall whether Agrippa had already known about heliocentrism, then she shouted, "Please stop that right now! If anyone comes in, I could lose my job, and for you, it could be even worse!"

Maarten closed his fist and the display abruptly ceased. Right at that moment, one of the Fellows came into the room. He was an older gentleman named Constantijn, who everyone in the College believed was going to retire next year, a belief that had held firm for as long as Johanna had worked at the College.

Constantijn, seemingly intending to ignore Johanna as she was only a Librarian and so far beneath his station, strode on to his favorite section. But then he stood still, looked around, and sniffed the air. He appraised his surroundings, sniffed again, and produced an ornate silver snuff box from his robes. He said, "Something smells very queer in here."

"I don't smell a thing," Johanna said truthfully.

"Still, there's something odd," Constantijn went on, closing the snuff box and putting it back into his pocket. "I think you ought to investigate and see if the students are not up to some mischief."

"Students aren't allowed in here," Johanna said.

"I know, but that hasn't stopped them from playing mischief before . . ." Constantijn's gaze went to Maarten, who had meanwhile walked over to a bookshelf further away and was pretending to be deeply engrossed in a book. "What's he doing here?"

"Oh, he's a Fellow from another College," Johanna said. "He's here to look at the collection of treatises on warfare."

"Most interesting, most interesting," Constantijn said. "The art of warcraft is a neglected art indeed! And this is such an interesting treatise by the Duke of Gelre. Back in my day, we would study these treatises, but now, alas, we are vulnerable and open to attack by the French. Don't think they won't come!"

Johanna felt fortunate that Constantijn's eyesight was failing. Even so, he was always in his own little world of letters and grand ideas and theories—there was simply no room in his mind for other people, their designs, or their lies.

Constantijn bid them both good day and left. Now, they were all alone. The air seemed quiet, almost hushed, as if it was waiting for them to do something else.

"Does magic smell?" Johanna asked.

"No, but I think he must have sensed it. He may possess a little bit of magical ability. I'm not sure," Maarten said.

"You know," Johanna said, "What do students do in libraries?"

"I don't know. Study?"

"We Scholars know better. I will show you." She pulled him gently in between the shelves and kissed him again.

MAARTEN

THE SIGNS APPEARED OVERNIGHT, plastered across the city of Haltra, the carp blazon indicating an official notice. Maarten read out the words to Cees, who could not read, and to Jelmer, who could but seemed unconcerned. The signs prohibited citizens from giving any alms to beggars and buskers, with a stiff fine of ten gulden for any trespassers. *Do your part to keep the city free of scroungers and tramps.*

In the weeks that followed the notices, Maarten's earnings dwindled. He shared what he had with Cees and Jelmer, but their pockets were just as empty. He cursed his decision to spend all his money on a clean shave and haircut at a professional barber, to have his new clothes washed, and to have a rotting tooth pulled by a decent dentist. What a waste, except for the tooth. He was still getting used to the mild taste of his own spit.

Romance be damned: it was expensive, and he could not afford it. Besides, he had not seen Johanna in days. He began to sense that all-too-familiar clawing hunger that he knew would soon become impossible to ignore: the persistent pangs of an empty stomach, severe headaches that seemed to come out of nowhere, the strange paper-dry lips, a horrible sickness that could only be blunted with large quantities of cheap alcohol. And the alcohol would also help him forget, at least for a little while . . .

He drew Rita from the memory of the painting he had seen in Johanna's boat. Her smile appeared to mock him. He must seek out Johanna. It was humiliating, but either that or starve.

JOHANNA

JOHANNA, MEANWHILE, had been working hard the past few weeks. She was cataloging the older Metaphysics collection of the library, stuffy, yellowing tomes that stood tightly packed on shelves.

She smiled as she dusted off Ficino's commentary to Aristotle's *On Magic*, a slim volume that no-one had requested for at least a quarter-century, judging by the dust it had collected. She mumbled: "No one studies magic anymore these days." The new science did not seem to have a place for it.

A young woman, fair-skinned with flaxen hair tied up in a severe bun, came in. She wore the dull gray, slightly frayed robes of the serving-women. She pulled a trolley into the room, stacked with more heavy books. She introduced herself as Kitty, the new assistant for the Librarian, and she would be in charge of the section on Metaphysics, Rhetoric, and Logic.

Johanna looked up in surprise. "Where is Loesje?"

Loesje had been Johanna's previous assistant, and she had only been working at the library for a few months. That girl had been outspoken, with sharp commentaries on the books. Very different from *this* little mouse of a girl, Johanna thought.

"Ah, Loesje, well . . . they had to let her go . . ." Kitty said, her eyes downcast.

"Really? Why?"

The new girl said nothing, but Gerrit Vandeveen, the Head Librarian, came in and answered instead: "Loesje had the gift of magic. We will have no kindle, flame, or magic in the library, and certainly none wielded by servants. Imagine an unlicensed Magician in this library, and the power they could unleash with all these ancient books!"

"What's wrong with Magicians?" Johanna objected, a protectiveness for Maarten welling up in her.

Gerrit surveyed the narrow, high-walled, book-cluttered room, which seemed even stuffier than usual with three people in it. "Well, there's nothing wrong with them *per se*, though I never trust a Magician. High *burgers* can be Magicians, and so can the nobles, of course . . . It is proper that those who inherit or purchase the tools of magic can wield their power. That's why we have licenses, to protect the public order. But imagine magic in the gray folk! Imagine your serving-man, or your scullery maid, as a magician!" (He seemed to have forgotten Johanna had neither.) "Magical ability in the gray is dangerous, it's like them having access to gunpowder. Or have you forgotten what's stirring up in France?"

Johanna opened her mouth to object. But Gerrit raised his hand to silence her. "I see, my dear Johanna, that you still have a lot of work to do. I'll let you get on with cataloging."

When she was left to herself with the stack of books, Johanna thought again about Maarten and wondered why she had not seen him for so many days.

Then it dawned on her. *The signs!* Of course.

Had Maarten been forced to leave Haltra? Would he leave without saying goodbye to her?

JOHANNA CAME OUTSIDE THAT NOON, her eyes adjusting from the permanent twilight of the library to the stark sun of high summer. She fully expected not to see Maarten. But there he stood, right outside the entrance, looking at her with wary intensity.

Her hand went up in a hesitating little wave. "My lungs are full of dust. Archival work." She coughed to emphasize the point, and with some difficulty stopped a subsequent stream of wheezing and retching.

She tried to regain her dignity while coughing up and swallowing her own dusty phlegm, while Maarten stood silently, all the while staring at her.

"Would you like us to buy sandwiches and then eat them outside on a bench?" she croaked at last. "I could do with some fresh air."

She bought him a sandwich, which he devoured in a

few quick bites. They then took a tour in the manicured gardens of the College. As he walked beside her, she noticed that Maarten seemed even thinner than before. He had lost his easy, supple gait and moved with considerable effort. The silence between them grew uncomfortable.

Johanna began, in a more accusatory tone than she intended, "Why are you homeless? You've got so much talent, why aren't you a famous Magician?"

"Why's anyone homeless?" He collapsed on an iron-work bench, "Do you think that being talented, or industrious, guarantees you don't become homeless? Or that everyone who lives on the streets is lazy or stupid?"

"No, I didn't mean to imply any of that!" Johanna said, reddening.

"To you housed folk, it must seem that us streetfolk are a lazy lot," he said, shifting to the edge of the bench. "You don't know what it's like or how we live. Take collecting gratuities. You have no idea, the work that goes into it."

"What do you mean?"

"Money is like seeds. You sow some in your collection box when you begin the day, and people will give you coins that resemble what's already there. Ideal is a doublet, or a few stuivers—and they multiply. I have to keep an eye on it to make sure there's not too much, also that it doesn't get stolen. But there can't be nothing, or nobody gives. You know what the worst thing is? When I have no money at all to seed the collection box myself. It can take hours before I get my first coin. But just as bad is when people give you their duiten—those work as magnets for more worthless copper. Try to go to any shop with that."

"How about gulden or ducatons?" Johanna asked.

"They're fine but cannot be used to seed. People see a ducaton and they'll say, 'He has plenty to get by already! Anything more and he'll buy liquor and drink himself into a stupor!' So, I have to monitor very carefully what the money looks like and how much there is. Not too little, so I don't look pathetic and undeserving, but not too much— cause otherwise I'd be *drinking myself to death*."

"I'm sorry," Johanna said. "I didn't know."

"Well, you didn't *need* to know."

"Speaking of which," Johanna hesitated. "I've seen those signs that tell us we shouldn't give to . . . people like you."

She edged a little bit closer to him, and grasped his hand, which felt cold and limp. She faltered, "What I'm trying to say is: are you alright?"

"I get by," Maarten said, gazing at his shoes, which had holes at the seams. A deep blue butterfly landed on a bright patch of purple flowers. They both looked at it for a while in silent wonder.

Johanna said, "What would it take for you to solve the problems you have?"

"It's nothing you can help with. You know that magical power is housed in old, expensive objects. I don't have access to those. Independent licensed Magicians have white-gold rings, set with precious stones such as sapphires or diamonds. *You* wouldn't be able to afford that on a librarian's salary, and I wouldn't accept such a gift from you. You see the bind I'm in." He stared gloomily into the distance, at the patches of colorful flowers.

"I've seen them, they sometimes come to the library. They wear these long, purple cloaks and those flashy signet rings. That's where they get their magical power from?"

"It amplifies the magic. The older the ring, the more powerful it is. Even one ring would cost me a fortune. A license would cost me another fortune and I'd need to travel far to get it." Maarten sighed. "But there aren't people without problems. You must have your own problems, I reckon."

They got up from the bench and made their way back to work. As Johanna waved goodbye to the college porter, she said, "Well, to be frank, I don't think I have problems. I am perfectly content. I like the way my life's going, I love my little boat. It wasn't always like this. I worked my arse off to get the Scholar's license. I sacrificed everything: friends, a social life, romance . . . I sat the exams so many times, I became the laughingstock in the examination halls. But I'm here now!"

"Perfectly content?" Maarten queried, right before they went their separate ways for the afternoon. "Perfect doesn't exist."

JOHANNA CARESSED THE SPINES of the incunabula housed in the Rare and Precious Books collection. This little room, all at the back of a larger room with periodicals, held exceptional manuscripts and rare books that only Scholars were allowed to see. They rarely did so anymore. Medieval books had become obsolete. Who cared about Aquinas if you could read Spinoza, Descartes, or even nowadays, Diderot and d'Alembert?

She looked with pleasure at the newly purchased volumes of Diderot and d'Alembert's *Encyclopédie* which cataloged the new science in twenty-eight splendid volumes, bound in elegant calf leather. *Knowledge will set you free.* Not long ago, precious books like these would have been chained with big iron shackles, to prevent Magicians from stealing them. The chains revealed something important about these ancient tomes. They were dangerous because of their inherent force, because of what some people could do with them. Would the *Encyclopédie* have magical properties? She had no idea. But Maarten would!

Johanna came to a decision. It was madness. It would upset everything she had worked for. But then she imagined Gerrit's mocking voice: "Magic in the gray is danger-ous, like gunpowder." She thought of Loesje who was fired, and of Maarten who, it was now plain to see, would starve if she did not intervene.

MAARTEN

T HE NEXT WEEK, as they were having their lunch at Carla's coffeehouse, Johanna handed Maarten a small brown parcel.

"This is so heavy . . . with magic, I mean. What is it?" he whispered.

She drew closer, her squat body leaning perilously on the tall chair like a little fat bird perched on a thin branch, and mumbled, "I'm probably going to regret this, but *verdomd*, I want to help you. It's a manuscript, rare and valuable. It's obviously not for you to keep forever. It's probably worth a thousand ducatons. But . . . I think it will help you with your work, if only for a couple of weeks or so. Please don't unpack it, it might get damaged."

Maarten felt he should refuse right away. Yet here was something that could solve perhaps not *all* his problems, but certainly his most immediate one of cash flow: a portable object that contained enough magic for him to draw on. As he held it, he could feel its force seep through, making him light-headed.

"How on earth did you get a thing like this? How do you even know it's got magic amplification?" he whispered.

"I have got my sources," Johanna said mysteriously.

"But how . . ." Maarten insisted, turning over the parcel in his hands as if the answer could be found on it.

"Ah well, a Magician came into the library a little while back. He didn't wear the robes but I could tell right away. Something in his demeanor, too many rings on his fingers, and he wanted to see the incunables and manuscripts. And he singled this one out as being very powerful. He even said to me, 'Be careful that it doesn't get lost, the magic that could be amplified out of this is enough to set the whole of Haltra ablaze.' "

Maarten was taken aback but put the parcel in his bag anyway.

"Handle it with care. Use it wisely, and give it back to me soon, before it is missed," Johanna said.

THAT AFTERNOON, MAARTEN FOUND a suitable spot to draw close to the Graslei, a long leafy lane along a canal where the wealthier citizens of Haltra would stroll from the Quarter That Trades to the Center That Rules. None of the regular buskers or beggars were in close proximity. He thought for a moment on what kind of scene would be best for the heavy magical powers he could amplify.

He drew a tempestuous ocean with a tall ship that struggled through the storm. The waves swept; seabirds cried in thin but convincingly desolate cries. The masts and billowing sails of the man-o-war almost disappeared behind a large blue-green wave, but it emerged unscathed, and was tossed about mercilessly. He drew a second ship with the pirate flag fully raised. Shots in chalk were fired, accompanied by soft pops.

The crowd grew ecstatic, and the donations poured in.

"A real Magician!" they cried with delight. Parents put their kids on their shoulders so they could get a clearer view in the jostling mass.

A little distance away, a man with a ruddy face and a white beard spread out a blanket that once must have been white. He took out a battered fiddle with a missing top string, and began to play a hoarse, squeaky melody: *Le Prisonnier de Hollande*. Though a catchy enough tune, this was apparently the only piece in his repertoire. On and on he went, with stoic determination, playing the piece in a soulless, mechanistic manner.

As the evening beams reddened the canal water, the fiddler approached Maarten. "What do ye think ye're doing?" he asked in a low voice.

"I'm here, same as you, what does it look like I'm doing?" Maarten said, hastily pocketing his earnings.

"Ye know what I'm talking about. Ye're depriving me and other hard-working artists of our earnings. Ye're monopolizing the audience. The rest of us ain't getting much since the signs!" The man had come very close now, his breath reeking of alcohol, unfocused despair in his pale eyes, looking more pitiful than menacing.

"I need to get by," Maarten said, keeping his voice free of pity.

The fiddle-player muttered, "I don't want to see ye here again, or I'll break all yer fingers, one by one. You try to draw then, Magician."

A jolt went through Maarten as he realized that, in fact, he *was* a Magician now. An unlicensed one. While this was not strictly illegal, he could still be charged with disruption of the public order through the unregulated use of magic. He idly wondered what the penalty was for that and considered it would probably not be a simple shoe-theft or beating.

MAARTEN WAS MORE THAN getting by. He had made more money in that week than he had for the entire duration of some summers.

"Own up. Did you steal a ring or something? What's going on?" Cees said, in that calm manner indicating he would not let the matter drop. The rain was hard and steady, but the wind's direction was favorable, and they remained dry under the bridge.

Sizzling in the pot was meat—not just any meat, *steak*. Neither of the three friends could remember when they had last eaten meat. Maarten turned over the steak filets, releasing the smell of fresh rosemary, the herbs making this dinner even more of an unseemly splurge.

Jelmer agreed. "You would never buy steak with your normal earnings—and now, well, nobody else ain't getting any money at all."

"I'm sharing though," he said, unwilling.

"Come on, are we friends, or ain't we?" Cees insisted. "Where's the money coming from?"

Maarten let the spoon rest atop the pot and took the parcel out of his bag. "This is an old book. Powerful magical amplification. Johanna gave it to me."

With a quick movement, Cees snatched the book away and tossed it to Jelmer, who began to unwrap it.

"Careful with that! It's delicate! It's raining!" Maarten warned, as he tried to get the book back in vain.

Jelmer continued to unwrap the paper methodically, revealing a worn, unassuming-looking book with a plain black cover. He opened it. They stared at the eruption of color, page after page of careful illuminations of Prophetesses garbed in deep ultramarine blue, carmine red, and delicate rose madder, with gold leaf borders. The glory of the Book of Hours was starkly offset against the gray and dirt of their surroundings.

"*Verdomd*, that book must be worth a fortune," Jelmer said in awe.

Cees shook his head. "You need to get that right back to where it came from. Are you out of your mind? If you get arrested, I don't know you."

The laws against witchcraft and sorcery, instituted centuries ago, were still in full force. But because magic was regulated through licenses now, it was rare to have a Magician burn at the stake. Often the charge would not be illegal magic, but disruption of the public sphere, or quackery. Whatever the charge, the outcome was bleak.

"Don't you worry, I'm going to return it first thing tomorrow," he promised.

But Maarten did not return the book that day, or the next day, as late summer came without incident.

Instead, he bought new clothes, including a pair of high-quality leather shoes. They were stiff, still uncomfortable, and too warm for the time of year, but they would be dry on the inside and protect his feet against the frost in winter. He saw Johanna every day and even paid for them to be able to meet in an inexpensive inn up in the Quarter That Works; her boat made him slightly seasick.

He basked in the luxury of romance; he allowed his thoughts to stray from bare necessities. Often there was a brief silence between them. He asked her, "Something's bothering you. What's wrong?" But she would smile and lie quietly in his arms, and say, "Nothing. I'm happy now. I used to be content, but it's not the same as true happiness."

He allowed that ray of happiness to also shine into his own, forever-preoccupied mind. How she must be debating within herself when to ask for the book back! Just a little longer. Just a few more weeks, and he'd have saved enough, he told himself.

JOHANNA

OHANNA DE VRIES HAD LEARNED the difference between *being content* and *happiness*. This was not because she required a man or sex to be happy, but because through being with Maarten, everything around her became deeper and more profound. She relished in simple things: the gentle patter of rain on the roof of her boat as a novel lay on her lap to be read with a cup of tea; the soft purr of Sammie by her side.

She also discovered something else: how marvelous it was to care about another human being and to see them do well. And Maarten did very well. He was still pale, but his clothes looked better, and he smelled better. "I smell funny," he protested when she convinced him to bathe in the new public bathhouse in the Center That Trades, the one with the marble steps and the fragrant towels. His shirts were crisp white, his hair was fashionably cut, and he was clean-shaven.

However, Johanna had not considered her next steps when she had stolen the Book of Hours. No-one had requested it. Maarten had not given any sign of wanting to return it.

One day, her colleague Hélène cooked up an idea that, under any other circumstance, would have delighted Johanna. The plan was to put the most beautiful books of the Library of the College of Liberal Arts on display for the public. Hélène and Mauritz talked it over in the senior common room.

Hélène sat leaning forward on a large, green velvet canapé, sipping from her cup of newly-imported jasmine tea. "A collection to stupefy and instill wonder in the people! Free and open to the public! We can show the maps of Africa and Asia with the travels of Maghelaes the Magician . . . a top piece. And that big Qur'an with the beautiful calligraphy, you know, the one from Isfahan . . ."

"Oh, and the Book of Hours," Mauritz interjected. "You are forgetting the Haltrean Book of Hours, which shows all the Prophetesses as they go about foretelling and working miracles."

"How could I forget?" Hélène cried, clapping her hands, nearly jumping out of her seat. "That book is spectacular! A wonder! A top piece."

A little distance away Johanna sat hunched over her small porcelain cup of too-strong coffee, hoping that her reddening ears would not be seen from that distance. How she despised Hélène and her talk of "top pieces," as if precious books were reducible to social reputation and ducatons!

"It is a noble plan," Mauritz considered, sitting down beside Hélène on the canapé. "But to put our beautiful, vulnerable books on display for the common folk is like throwing pearls to swine. Have you thought about insurance? Also, don't forget that many of these books have very strong magical properties, and you would not want them to end up in the hands of the wrong people!"

"Ah, Mauritz, you spoilsport! Let's ask our dear colleague, shall we?" Hélène's high voice rung through the common room even though the wooden paneling was designed to muffle sound. "Oh Johanna? Please be a dear and come over here!"

Johanna turned around slowly, her cup trembling on its saucer.

"Come over here, we wish to hear your opinion, old girl!" she cried, exuding insincere familiarity.

Johanna got up from her plush red chair and walked over to seat herself on an ottoman close to Hélène and Mauritz.

"In your opinion, should the gray be allowed to see our most precious books?"

"Books? I don't know. I don't know they'd be interested," Johanna mumbled, staring into her cup.

"Come on, Johanna," said Mauritz indulgently, "You are a *Librarian,* after all; you must have opinions on this matter. Do you think it's a good idea for any Jan, Cees, or Rick to see your most precious books? Do you think Gerrit is right that they would start a revolution?"

"It hardly seems likely," Johanna said. "The knowledge

or the magic contained in books did not start the stirrings in France, though I know there were some magicians on the front lines."

"So," Hélène interjected, "in your opinion, how did they do it? If not through magic, why is the revolution happening in France? Why now, why there?"

"Hope," Johanna answered firmly. "Hope is stronger than any magic. They did it because of their firm belief that things can be changed."

"Well, Johanna, you would know all about that, wouldn't you," Mauritz said as he got up from the canapé. "You've taken away my reservations. If *hope* is what's fueling the French revolution, I don't see why we can't open our books to the public. You can help to organize it, Johanna. Pick some of the finest manuscripts and make an inventory of, say, about thirty works. We will review it. Make sure to include the Qur'an, the Moon book and the Book of Hours. Don't forget the highlights."

"Thank you," Johanna said without warmth. *Why can't I just shut my* verdomde *mouth and stop arguing with these people?* she wondered. She'd have to ask Maarten to return the book. There was no other option.

Maarten

Y EARS AGO, CEES HAD TOLD Maarten that you
make your own justice on the streets. "In fact," he
opined, "streetfolk have the advantage here!
Housed folk have to wait for the slow wheels of justice to
turn their way. They need magistrates, courthouses, and
cleaning crews. For us, justice is immediate."

One sunny late summer's day, Maarten drew a large
pond that reflected the tall and ancient Belfry at the edge of
the Quarter That Trades and the Center That Rules, sur-
rounded by a blue, cloudless sky. Inside the pond crowded
a flurry of red, orange, black and white goldfish. He invited
passersby to put their hands close to the chalk water-sur-
face. The fish appeared to approach, creating widening

white chalk circles around their mouths. People pretended to feed the fish and laughed in delight. The money (almost all stuivers and even some gulden) streamed in.

As he put away his chalks, three disheveled figures approached: the old fiddler with the white beard, a stringy-looking bald man with bloodshot eyes, and a middle-aged woman in rags who he had seen begging before.

"I warned ye," the fiddler said. "Get out of my spot, or face the consequences."

Maarten said in what he hoped was a conciliatory tone: "Please don't come any closer. I don't want to harm you. You've seen, I am a powerful Magician, and I won't hesitate to defend myself." Meanwhile he thought frantically, *defend myself how, exactly?* He looked around for anything to use as a shield or weapon.

"If ye want to do what's fair, share what ye have with us," the woman pleaded. "I'm starving since the signs! We *all* are, except ye. It ain't right!" She wasn't joking. Her once-puffy cheeks were sallow and sunken.

As Cees had advised, once you give in to threats there's no end to it. So Maarten said, "Sorry, I'm saving up."

"Saving up for *what*?" the old man asked, bewildered, the concept of saving completely alien to him.

It was for a ring. A Magician's ring that would grant him the same abilities as the Book of Hours.

"Now don't be selfish, just hand over yer cash," said the bald man, approaching him.

Maarten felt the resolve rise within him as he said, "No, I *won't*. Ye ought to blame Haltra's City Council, not me. And I'm under no obligation to subsidize ye."

Near the Belfry stood an empty cart that was used for transporting vegetables. It floated purposefully toward the three assailants. The bald man backed away. But the woman's despair triumphed over her fear. She brandished a long, thin knife. "Yer cash."

The cart flew forward at speed, past her hand holding the knife, hitting the stained-glass window of a nearby apothecary. The beautifully wrought serpent and cup shattered instantly. They heard the rattling wheels and hooves of a large carriage approaching. The group of three dashed away, and Maarten grabbed his bag and ran. Staying in Haltra had become impossible.

JOHANNA

MAARTEN HAD DISAPPEARED without warning, and Johanna was worried on the first day of his absence. This wasn't like him at all, not anymore. She felt a visceral sense of longing. It wasn't just that Maarten was gone; all her familiar surroundings seemed out of sorts.

On the second day of Maarten's absence, Johanna's thoughts shifted from him to the book she had stolen for him. What would happen if its disappearance was noticed? She began to dread requests from the rare manuscript archives. Dark thoughts began to cloud her mind. What had she been thinking? Making new friends was already impossible at her age, let alone romance. She was nearing *fifty*.

Had Maarten only used her to gain access to the book? What if it was found out? Everything she had ever worked for would go up in smoke. All those years of studying, all those years of stoically bearing the scorn of others. Why had she reached for happiness when she had a perfectly good situation?

Worse, there was no way to discreetly look for someone she knew nothing about. Not even his last name, or where he was from. Late summer rolled into fall and students returned to the Colleges, their robes flowing in the autumn breeze as they walked by in pairs, discussing natural philosophy or mechanical science.

Despite the city's prohibition, Johanna did give to beggars and street performers, especially as winter drew in and frost hung in the air. Whenever she met an unhoused person at the side of the street, she took the time to make eye contact and smile. They would nod and smile back, happy for the acknowledgement and the cash. "Thank ye kindly, ma'am," and "The Prophetesses bless ye."

Johanna had to bite her tongue to not reply: "What do the Prophetesses have to do with it? They certainly didn't bless you!" But what could she say? These people had hopes, and dreams and talents, just like everyone else. And they had their own place in the economy of Nature, just like everyone. They were just as much a part of Haltra as the students who gathered in the courtyards, or the sparrows who ate the students' leftovers once they settled into their rooms in the evenings, or the Tutorial Fellows who taught the students, and the librarians who took care of their study materials.

"Some librarian am I, I can't even keep my books in good order," she mumbled to herself, as she set off to her narrowboat for the night.

MAARTEN

MAARTEN HADN'T THOUGHT it was possible for a drifter to feel adrift. This was doubly strange since he had—for the first time in his life, really—a clear goal beyond the immediate pursuits of obtaining food and shelter. This was his plan: save enough money, buy a ring, give the book back to Johanna, buy a Magician's license, find his starving friends, help them. With the license, he could become an independent Mage (he guessed, probably correctly, that wage labor would not suit him).

The temporary shelters he had had with Cees and Jelmer, the makeshift camps they set up whenever they came into a new city, often under a bridge or in some ruined building, had always felt like "home." They were spaces where you belonged. A place where you weren't judged or ignored. Now he was sleeping under a bridge by himself. He often thought about his traveling companions. It came naturally to him to imagine their remarks, their replies, even their comments on his cooking as he sat all by himself making a makeshift dinner with some newly bought cooking utensils. With a pang in his stomach, his thoughts also turned to Johanna.

"You shouldn't have done that!" he shouted to the stars as he cooked beans over an open fire, "You really shouldn't. I didn't ask for it!" His voice echoed over the water of one of the canals of Ghandia. Ghandia was a large and handsome city, a few days' journeys away from Haltra. It was his new place, the local *burgers* were interested in his chalk art and paid well, but it didn't feel like home, not the way Haltra had.

Now he always had enough to eat. Showing his magical displays and pocketing the earnings, slowly he was accumulating some wealth. His fingers and nails were no longer caked with filth mixed with chalk. They looked lean and delicate, like the bourgeois hands of a Scholar, maybe even a Magician. He visited bathhouses regularly; the smell of salts had now become familiar. His entire standard of cleanliness had shifted. But he was still a long stretch away from acquiring a ring. A quality silver or white-gold ring would cost at least sixty ducatons. His best shot would be at one of the main auction houses.

Some weeks later, Maarten set off with his gaze firmly set upon the rising North Star. It would guide him northeast to the city of Anversia, a cosmopolitan northern port town with several auction houses. It took him three marches, but they wound pleasantly through the countryside, and he could walk them in comfortable, soft, yet strong, leather shoes. His step was free and light, and the moon was almost full, illuminating his path.

LIGHT FILTERED THROUGH the beer-colored windows of the Veilingzaal, where goods were auctioned off every Friday afternoon. Dust motes drifted lazily in slanting golden beams of the late afternoon sun, which cast a steady glow on the rugs, furniture, paintings and jewelry on display.

Maarten had recently arrived in Anversia. In the Zaal he could discern the hubbub of different languages. His ear immediately picked up French, though he had not spoken it in over a decade, in addition to Dutch and Flemish. The Veilingmeester had the dark skin and fine curly hair of people from Africa beyond the Great Desert. Maarten discerned the distinct guttural sounds of Arabic, reminiscent of Dutch. This was where the whole world seemed to meet. There was a pleasant busyness all around the city.

He noticed another Magician in the Zaal. He felt her presence the moment he walked in: a young woman with the dark wavy hair of the Arabs. Like him, she did not wear the purple magician's cloak, but unlike him, she probably had a license. She wore several rings on her right hand, all wrought white gold. She gave him a long, searching, somewhat haughty look. It made sense to be incognito. Auctions were the rare occasions where one might be able to buy magical objects at a bargain price.

The Veilingmeester made a sign to the public that the

auction would begin soon, and that they should get their numbered boards. A young man wearing smart black velvet asked: "I saw a rug hidden behind that cabinet. Is that for sale?"

The Veilingmeester said, "Aha, sir, I see you are a connoisseur of Oriental crafts. Yes . . . I was not sure if I should sell this masterpiece, given how small this group is. Few people can gauge the worth of this magnificent cloth. Twenty-seven million knots, superb Ottoman craftsmanship! Look at the brightness of those flowers, the intricacy! But now that you have seen it, I have no choice but to put it up for auction, though I will likely make a loss if I sell it here." The Veilingmeester shrugged and beckoned to his helpers, two teenage boys, to lift the rolled-up rug and unroll it over the floor.

People stood around, admiring the fine handiwork. Maarten marveled at the Veilingmeester's abilities. The trick with the partially hidden carpet had not escaped him. Such skillful management of sentiment was akin to magic.

But Maarten had no interest in rugs or crockery. His eye had been caught by a white-gold ring, with a simple but clear sapphire set in it. It drew him with the irresistible force that all magical objects did, and within him welled a strong desire to pick up the ring and slip it on his finger. It was often said that a ring chooses its bearer—whether this was mere lore or fact, it definitely felt like it was true in this case.

"I see you know your jewelry," the Veilingmeester said, having approached Maarten with a few silent strides. Maarten evaded his searching look, and mumbled: "I am looking for a gift, for a dear friend."

"That person is lucky to have you for a friend. This is an exquisite ring. Eighteen karats, that is the best standard for white gold, as you undoubtedly know. And look how elegant the setting is. It's a small man's ring, but I can have it sized for a woman too."

Maarten received a small wooden board with the number "26" on it and chose a seat near the exit on one of the low, wooden benches. The auction began. Objects that no-one was interested in were quickly ushered out. Objects that garnered interest elicited a carefully orchestrated series of theatrics from the Veilingmeester. He groaned, "Honestly, I cannot believe I am letting this go for thirty ducatons! You all will be the ruin of me!"

The rugs were carried out of the room, and the Veilingmeester signaled the next batch of objects to be sold. "Now onto jewelry. We start with this beautiful white-gold ring with a sapphire setting. White gold, as you know, has mercury in the setting. And that is why Magicians prize these rings!"

Maarten knew this. Mercury was one of the alchemical metals that, when combined with gold, gave an object its magical force in ways that the new science still could not explain.

The Veilingmeester held the ring between his dark thumb and index finger, allowing the sunlight to catch it as he showed it to the audience. "Now imagine, dear customers, that you could be the owner of such a timeless, magical piece of jewelry! I see the lady at the front is very interested in this ring! Let's start the bidding at . . ."

"Fifteen ducatons," the female Magician in the front said.

"Fifteen. Do we have a second bid?" the Veilingmeester asked. "Nobody? A reminder to this audience that we need a second bid to sell this ring!"

The Meester shifted his gaze to the edge of the room and acknowledged Maarten's first bid. "I see twenty . . . Now, twenty-five for the lady."

The bidding went on. Maarten carried his entire fortune, which was exactly seventy ducatons, on his person. He tried to relax. There would be other opportunities, plenty of them. He was in Anversia, the city of trade and commerce. The whole city was one giant Quarter That Trades.

But he wanted *this* ring. He had never felt such a strong desire for an object in his entire life. The world shrank to the size of the ring's diameter. He broke out in a sweat. He wore an elegant waistcoat in smooth satin. It felt suffocating now, as sweat ran down his back.

"Fifty-five for the gentleman at the back," the Veilingmeester continued. "Sixty for the lady in the front. Do I hear sixty-five?"

Maarten's board went up without hesitation. In this game, you do not flinch; you do not let on where you stand. "Sixty-five for the lady in the front."

Maarten put up the board one final time. "Seventy. Going once, going twice . . . Oh . . . seventy-five for the lady."

Maarten was outbid. Shattered, he rose to his feet and left, not caring how undignified he looked.

Outside, Maarten took a deep breath of the faintly saline air. He walked by the quay to watch the well-provisioned packet boats come into Anversia's harbor. He tried to shake his disappointment, and with it his lingering desire for the ring. All things considered, his situation was not bad. He had all his money, still. There would be another opportunity. But not for this ring! He had so strongly sensed that they were meant to be together. He shook his head again, trying to rid himself of that feeling.

A clear woman's voice from behind asked in smooth Flemish with an Arabic accent: "If you, hypothetically, had won the ring, what would you have done with it?"

He turned around and saw the female magician standing a little distance away. She now wore a Magician's cloak, and all the fingers of her right hand were ringed. The new ring was clearly too big for her little finger. She would get it resized later, he reckoned.

"What is that to you? It looks splendid. A very good day to you," he said, not caring at all for conversation, or to indulge her in her gloating.

"I know. It is a good ring. I was thinking . . . perhaps you need it more than me? Perhaps this really *is* your ring. I had a feeling . . . but I need to know what you would do with it once you have this ring, as I assume it would be your first?" She stood to face him, and he felt somewhat intimidated though she was a full head shorter than he was.

"I'd buy a license next, and become an itinerant artist and Mage," he said stiffly.

"That's fine, but is that it?" she asked. "Nothing more?"

"What more should I do?" he asked. The auction had concluded in the meantime, and people were streaming out of the Zaal in small groups, servants carrying rugs under their arms, balancing crockery in precarious baskets, schlepping along large and small pieces of furniture.

"You could use it for good," she suggested. "Magic is subversive. It holds the power to change the world. You see, anyone could be born with the powers of a Magician. But you also need to have the *mind* of the Magician. I mean not someone who obeys the set order, I mean someone who is their own master."

Maarten very much wished to end this pointless conversation. He said: "I don't know what you mean by 'the mind of the magician.' I ain't beholden to the set order. I've lived on the streets for a long time now and been my own master. I obey no-one."

A flock of seagulls passed overhead. The magician looked up. "That's all very fine, but obeying no-one still doesn't convince me that you having the ring would be better than me having the ring."

Maarten did not want to say that he needed it more than her. Whatever he said, he would not beg. He had never resorted to begging and he sure as hell would not begin now. "Sure," he said sourly. "As I said, it looks great on you. Have a fine rest of your day."

He began to turn around, but she said, "Wait a moment! I am willing to sell you my newest ring for seventy ducatons, though I am saddened to part with such a fine piece of jewelry. But I have a condition. Think about what you can do with this power, and how you can use it for good. Think about how magic should benefit not just you, but also others."

Maarten nodded and promised he would do so. He was still expecting her to change her mind as he counted out the ducatons into her elegant palm. In the distance, a large three-mast ship came into the harbor. Seagulls cried and landed in large groups to wait for the bounties the vessel would bring. The cold breeze felt refreshing and temperate. It was a beautiful day.

Finally, he could return the book. Even if he never did any great deeds like the magician wanted from him, he could at least put Johanna's mind at ease.

JOHANNA

OR THE FIRST TIME in her unremarkable career, Johanna faced a first disciplinary hearing. Three Scholars, the minimum number for a Quorum, sat opposite her at a long table. She fidgeted with her hair and suppressed the urge to bite her nails, a nasty habit she had never got rid of. She knew all of them—Gerrit of course, and two other senior Fellows. The loss of the book had finally been discovered through a request from a reader. When her worst fears came true, what she felt was—most of all—relief.

Johanna insisted she didn't know where the book was. She kept her head lowered and protested with fervor the high turnover of personnel and understaffing at the library.

"Cataloging in the new system is already a full-time job. I'm there working a three-man job all alone, and I've only got one assistant. How could I possibly keep a lookout for thieves?" she asked.

"It is your responsibility as head librarian," Gerrit insisted. "If you can't keep the books in order, what are you even doing?"

"Maybe it is just misplaced?"

"You had better find it back then. Your deadline is exactly two months from now. If you cannot find the book within that time, I'm afraid you'll have to compensate the Library or offer your labor for free in lieu of compensation. Of course, given the value of the book and your salary, that latter option isn't realistic."

"I'll find the book," Johanna said.

THERE WAS NO WAY to find the book. Johanna sat in her little boat, Sammie purring on her lap, thinking she should unmoor the boat and go on a wild chase around the country, from city to city, to find Maarten.

"Have you seen a magician who makes beautiful chalk art?" she would ask in these fantasies. "Oh yes, he lives right there," they would say. And then they'd meet. He'd have some compelling explanation for why he had never bothered to look for her. He'd been ill, or otherwise incapacitated. She imagined she would spot one of his drawings in some faraway city, his unmistakable style, and then she could track him down. But those ideas vanished as she considered that it would be impossible to take leave now, and she wasn't sure she even remembered how to steer her boat properly.

But one morning in early spring, just a few days short of her deadline, Johanna saw an unfamiliar, tall blond man, wearing a long overcoat, boots, and an elegant wide-brimmed hat, standing waiting at the main visitor's entrance of the Library.

"Excuse me, madam, are you Johanna de Vries? I am Cees, I'm Maarten's secretary. He may have talked about me. You gave him something on loan. He don't need it anymore, so I am returning it to you." He handed her a brown parcel. The weight and size indicated this was the Book of Hours. Cees added, as Johanna struggled to keep her passions under control, "Also, he's real sorry he borrowed the book for so long. He hopes you can forgive him."

"Where is he?" she asked.

"I'm sorry, I can't tell you anything more," the man replied. Giving her one final compassionate searching look, he walked off.

Johanna did not wait until the hearing, which was scheduled for the end of the week. Instead, she went to Gerrit and told him triumphantly that she had found the book while reorganizing a section for the cataloging work. Though it felt shameless, she added that the book incident showed she needed another assistant besides Kitty, at least for the duration of the reorganization and cataloging. Gerrit allowed her a second assistant. In this way, to Johanna's surprise, the unpleasant incident left her better off than before. The new assistant was a girl named Maryse, a tall, broad-hipped maid with strawberry blond hair who looked like she belonged in the countryside rather than in a library, but who was remarkably efficient and diligent.

For Johanna, the return of the book ended a long, drawn-out chapter in her life. Her time with Maarten seemed like a dream, which only became real and solid in the wee hours of the night when she woke up and could not get back to sleep. She would get up and try to shake the feeling by making herself a cup of tea. *He has a secretary now? And yet, he can't be bothered to visit me? He just gave me back the book, and that's it?*

Sammie was delighted by his mistress' new night routine. He begged for food, at first cautiously, then more and more brazenly. She took some dried fish out of the pantry and gave it to him, and he rewarded her with a big cuddle and a huge purr. Johanna drank her tea, hands clasped around her mug, stroking Sammie's head. It seemed easier now to not think of Maarten at all. Several hours could go by without a single thought of him. His face no longer haunted her mind. Their relationship was truly over.

Maarten

THERE IS A KIND OF background trust that things will turn out well. A feeling that not only Nature, but your personal life's ultimate end, arcs towards the good. This feeling does not require faith or belief. It is more fundamental than that.

Maarten lost that feeling when he lost everything. It happened thirteen years ago, in the French countryside, when Maarten was still called Martin. He and his father owned a flock of sheep, fine beasts with choice fleece they sold to Flemish carders at a fair price. For shepherds they were well off and they were happy together, just the two of them. Maarten's father could even afford to send him to school so he could learn to read, write, and do the accounts.

The schoolmaster admired the boy's skills with paints and chalks, and tentatively asked his father if he might not consider an apprenticeship at a local workshop. But his father said firmly, "No, we are shepherds through and through," not asking his son's opinion.

His father played a thin reed flute as they watched the stars at night, marveling over the vast constellations, and the delicate pinks and rose madders of the Milky Way. When it was raining, snowing, or too cold to be outside, they stayed in the shepherd's hut, comfortable, small, near their prized animals.

That all changed one day when the sheep startled and ran in panic over a cliff, crashing to their deaths. Father and son had to take wage labor, doing the same job they had done before as shepherds, but for low pay in the service of a nearby gentleman farmer. His father never played his flute again, and took to drinking their meager earnings away. He died just two years later.

Maarten handed in his notice and moved to a small city in the Low Countries to try and make his living as an artist. He had always loved drawing and sketching, but not being born to a guild family and not being wealthy, had found no way to express his talent.

After several days of wandering, he found an abandoned building, an old glassblowing workshop. It was occupied by two Dutchmen who appeared to be lovers, and their names were Cees and Jelmer. They were patient with his limited language skills in Dutch. They gave him shelter, blankets and a bowl of bland soup they had cooked on a makeshift stove in one of the old glass ovens.

"If you are to stay here," Cees said, "I need to know, what can you contribute? We don't do any favors for free here on the streets. It's give and take."

"I can draw," Maarten replied. "And I can cook, a little." (The soup had been truly awful.)

And so Maarten found his community, he became their cook and their artist. In the proximity of ancient objects and buildings, he was able to use his magical ability, but it was hard to find objects through which he could amplify magical power. He felt then that life, or Nature, does not arc toward the good—but if you rely on your talent and your friends, you can try to withstand the worst life can throw at you.

Cees, Jelmer, and he became a tight team. Maarten made street art. Jelmer had the most profitable venture. He would swindle people, putting on the best clothes he could find after many hours of scavenging through trash. He'd tell them he was a nobleman, down on his luck. He told hapless passersby he needed only *one* gulden or ducaton to pay off the debts his irresponsible elder brother had made. Jelmer had surmised that people's empathy for fallen nobles was far greater than for streetfolk who never stood a chance. And Jelmer had an aristocratic face, with large green eyes and dark, messy hair. He didn't look like someone who didn't get enough to eat, but like someone who simply didn't care for such mundane things as food.

Cees's main talent was to keep the little group organized. He cheered them up when things were hard, he tempered their enthusiasm and urged caution when things went well. Maarten would sometimes look at the pair with envy as they sat together wrapped in blankets. Love was possible, after all, even under these circumstances.

Now, with the ring, Maarten felt himself slip back into

the mindset from before he lost the flock, his fortune, and his father. Not only did he feel protected from life's vicissitudes, but somehow even blessed. How else to explain the magician who had sold him the ring? Or the Book of Hours Johanna was willing to lend him?

No, there's no such thing, he told himself. *Fortune is fickle. You're never safe.*

WITH THE RING on his finger, the next step of his plan presented itself. To find his old friends back and help them. He made inquiries; he asked the local street folk in all their old haunts. He traveled swiftly from city to city by postal carriage, and the weather improved. His new shoes were not even worn yet, the leather still intact. Finally, he was directed to an old bridge where he found Cees. Not a trace of Jelmer.

Cees was bundled up in his warmest winter clothes, a figure made bulky by layers and layers of fabric. He wore a thick, woolen overcoat that once might have looked beautiful and stylish, but even Maarten had never seen it in that state. He sat near an open fire that had run its course, staring into its embers.

"Oh, fancy seeing *you* here, if it isn't Maarten the Great Magician," he said with ironic emphasis.

"Where's Jelmer?"

Cees remained silent and continued to gaze into the dying fire.

"Where is he?" Maarten insisted.

"Jelmer's gone. He got a cold, then pneumonia. There was nothing I could do for him," Cees said simply.

"Oh no . . . I'm sorry,"

"Of course you are," Cees said. "That book and your magical talent could've come in mighty handy while we were, you know, *starving.* Or you could've taken us along on your ventures. Maybe, just maybe, Jelmer would still be here. We'll never know, I guess."

Maarten wanted to protest. He wanted to say, "I don't know how to do any healing magic!" or "I had to leave quickly because of a cleaning crew situation. But I came back as soon as I could!"

Instead, he knelt down, and only managed to say: "I'm sorry! I'm sorry! You should not have stayed in Haltra. The signs . . ."

"Don't you think there were signs elsewhere?" Cees replied. "Seems like there was a big campaign to starve us out, all across the Low Countries."

Maarten buried his hands in his face and said nothing. Cees got up with difficulty and put an awkward arm around his friend, saying gruffly, "There now, don't cry. That's not going to solve anything."

"I want to make it right," Maarten said. "I won't let you down again, I promise."

"How exactly are you going to do that?" Cees said. He surveyed Maarten critically, appraising his expensive clothes, his warm scarf.

"I can't bring Jelmer back, but I could employ you. You know that independent Magicians need personal secretaries."

"Some secretary I'd make. I can't even read or write," Cees scoffed.

"We can fix that. Reading and writing is easy. I'll teach you."

A MAGICIAN AND HIS SECRETARY sat facing each other at an elegant walnut table in a coffeehouse in Anversia. The establishment was splendid and large. It had an ample selection of drinks, and it boasted an elaborate glass-stained window, depicting the Apple Goddess and the Prophetess Blanceflor in their first encounter. The Apple Goddess handed the Prophetess a bright golden apple which granted her the second sight. Behind them stood an artfully wrought apple tree, representing the Original Orchard from which all wisdom about the workings of Nature stems.

Maarten looked at the work in an appreciative spirit as he faced the window, sipping his cocoa, savoring the sweetness mingled with bitterness in his mouth. Since that first cup Johanna had given him, he had slowly warmed to coffee, but never quite loved it the way other people did. Cees had fallen in love with coffee, waxing on about different varieties of beans and roasts, now drinking his third little cup of strong brew.

"Imagine if we had coffee back when! Better than liquor! Coffee can really get you through anything," he enthused. Behind Maarten sounded the steady, animated clicks of a billiard game in progress.

Maarten nodded and took another sip. They were incognito, as Maarten had not yet obtained the license for an independent Mage, but their arrival had still turned heads since they looked like young wealthy travelers, with comfortable but elegant clothing—ambassadors or diplomats.

There was the visible chain of Cees's brand-new silver pocket watch. Cees produced it, squinted at the face and said, after some mental calculation, "A quarter past two. I think we are done here. Where next? Several good hours of daylight, we can get our luggage at the inn and still leave today."

"We should arrange passage to Albion," Maarten said. "I hate traveling on boats, but that's where most of the Magician's societies are located and I really need that license if we are to get the best commissions."

"We could," Cees considered. "But right now, we're not that far from Haltra, and I've been thinking you ought to return that book to your girlfriend. It's been a few weeks since you got the ring, and you still haven't given the book back."

Maarten scowled. "She ain't my girlfriend anymore."

"Regardless." Cees finished his cup and beckoned the serving-woman for another one. "She might be in difficulty because of it. You've got to make things right, even if you never speak to her again."

Maarten sighed. He had considered it, of course. But he really could not face Johanna. It had become more and more difficult to envisage what such an encounter would look like and what she would say to him, how she would confirm all his worst thoughts about what she might be thinking about him.

After more animated clicking, one of the billiard players cried out, "I won! You owe me that fine hat now!"

"Tell you what," said Cees, "I'll do it. I'll go to Haltra tomorrow morning by postal carriage. It's just a couple of hours' travel. I'll explain. You don't need to meet her if you don't want to."

It felt like an easy way out. But Maarten said: "You would do that for me?"

"It's one of the tasks of a Magician's secretary to help them avoid awkward encounters with former lovers. I'll do it," Cees said.

When the book was returned, Maarten and Cees traveled to Albion by barge. It was more difficult to obtain the license than it had been to buy the ring. A license required an eyewitness and a fellow Magician to vouch for you. Maarten was turned away several times, until he found an old magician who didn't care about social decorum to help him. He passed all the standard tests: fire magic, concealment, transformation, and conjuring.

In the months that followed, Maarten and Cees continued to travel and work on commission. Maarten's talent attracted the attention of very wealthy patrons, and he could afford to become more selective about commissions he accepted.

Sometimes when he looked at Cees, he discerned not

so much his friend who was still alive, but the keen absence of his other friend. Cees and Jelmer had presented to him an ideal—the pair had struggled, fought, nearly starved on several occasions, but all the while, they had each other. Until they didn't.

THE HOMELESS MAN SEEMED DAZED; a bruise was already darkening across his cheek. He did not give in without a fight, but he was outnumbered. He stood on one bare foot, as he was taking off his second shoe and would hand it over to one of the uniformed men. The cleaning crew were about to jostle him into one of their black carriages. Cees and Maarten stood watching as the small drama unfolded in a back alley. On the dirt floor lay an old fiddle. One of the crew carelessly kicked it aside.

"Just keep moving, it's not your fight," Cees mumbled, gently pulling Maarten aside.

"I can't watch this and do nothing." Maarten took out his tinderbox and struck a small flame. He willed the flames outward and upward onto the lacquered wood of the closed vehicle. Fire magic still didn't come naturally to him, but it had the desired effect. The horses reared and panicked, pulling the carriage forward. The crew members looked up in astonishment, released their victim, and ran after the blazing carriage.

Cees picked up the fiddle. "Here's your instrument. Let's get you looked after, and we'll get you a new pair of shoes."

As they stood waiting in the apothecary while the pharmacist tended to the stranger's injuries, Cees said, "It's my job, as a Magician's secretary, to tell you you're being reckless. License or no, you can be still charged with disruption of the public order. Are you going to risk everything we've built so far, for someone we don't even know? Have some consideration for me, will you?"

"I can't believe you are so heartless," Maarten said. "Besides, I made a promise to the seller of this ring. I promised I wouldn't just use the magic for my own benefit."

"I get that," Cees said, staring out of the stained-glass window of the apothecary, which caught the sun, becoming brilliant prisms of green, blue, and red. "But what they're doing to street folk, it's an injustice—it's the whole of society. You can't fix that on your own. Not even if you were the most powerful Magician in the world, you couldn't. I guess that's why what's happening in France . . . *Give me liberty, equality, and brotherhood, or give me death,* that's one of their slogans."

Maarten sat down and looked outside, pondering. Maybe they should move; maybe they should start their own revolution here in the Provinces? Maybe the French revolutionaries would come and save them from the oppressors? He suddenly felt weary.

"So I'm supposed to just live while this is going on? While innocent people are beaten up on the streets, because they're poor? Live my life, be merry?"

"Well, that's what them housed folk seem to be doing all along, and they don't seem to have a problem doing that. A little scrap of happiness, it's the best you can hope for."

JOHANNA

THE NEXT WINTER, Johanna had reached a point where she seldom thought of Maarten at all. The cataloging job was finally done. She had been able to convince the Library management that Maryse, the new girl, should stay on as her assistant. *New girl*—what was she thinking, it had been almost a year!

But there was a problem. The plum tree had regrown.

When Johanna came in early in the morning and saw it on her way to work, a small group of people had already gathered around to watch. On the bench next to the tree, a small envelope was stuck against the leaning. Inside it was a note in a regular cursive she had only seen once, but instantly recognized. It said:

"Dear Johanna, I'm feeling in a better place right now so I can apologize properly to you. I'm sorry for leaving unannounced the way I did. Cees told me you received the book in good order. Meanwhile, I've been fine. Thanks to your loan, I could collect enough earnings to buy a ring powerful enough for my purposes. I also obtained a license, so I am a properly licensed independent Magician. I'm dreadful sorry I kept the book so long. I hope it didn't cause you trouble."

He was here, in Haltra? How? She looked up from the bench, expecting to see him, but of course, he wasn't there anymore.

Maarten and Johanna

As he left Appelgaard Inn, one of the very best inns in the Quarter That Trades, Martin des Prez (Or Maarten Vander Weyden as he was now known) reflected on his transformation. He was still the same person, but he had gone from being invisible to being all too visible. Wearing the recognizable purple cloak of a licensed Magician, people stared at him without restraint, pointing him out to each other. He was still figuring out the appropriate social response to this.

He felt alienated from the streetfolk. He always had a stash of doublets and stuivers to give to them; he owed them that much. Yet as he saw them just sitting there at the side of the road, in their layers of clothes and in their nests of useless rubbish, he had to push away an incipient sense of disgust. He knew they did this to conserve their energy, but it infuriated him to see them like that. *So that's how it begins.* He floated between worlds.

In any case, there weren't many people out today, since it was raining, as it had been the past few days. A good time to meet his clients. Cees was still asleep, which made it easier and less awkward. Cees always wanted to be so helpful that it felt counterproductive sometimes.

He pulled his cloak closer around him and adjusted his hat so the rim would catch most of the rain. Rain bothered him more now than it used to, and it felt icy on his skin. *You're growing soft.*

A figure in the distance approached in a purposeful manner at a brisk pace—a short, fat woman with a mass of red hair. His background sense of dread leapt to the foreground, tasting sour like the rotting tooth once had.

"How did you find me?" he asked, not looking in her direction.

"Ha! How did I find you? Your friend, sorry, your secretary, came to my boat and told me where you were. He said you would have left a note and would never come to see me, so he wanted to help things along a little."

They stood at the side of Hoornstraat, a broad street running through the Quarter That Studies and the Quarter That Trades in a north-south direction, with a handsome bridge arching over the Broadlei. The rain poured down mercilessly, mixed with sleet, and the wind picked up as though a fine storm was brewing.

"I'm here to do a wedding. They're a wealthy couple, and magical animated displays are in fashion now . . . Look, I'm sorry. I really am. I just..." Maarten searched for the words. "I wanted for us to be more equal."

In spite of the rain and sleet, in spite of the fact that they were both soaked, Johanna noticed immediately how much better Maarten looked than he had at any point during their acquaintance. This made it easier for her to get angry at him. "So you stole the book and left without saying a word."

"I gave it back though! But I thought it was an opportunity to save enough money to buy a ring, buy myself out of this crap, so I could be independent. But then, when I was finally able to, I couldn't face you. I didn't want to take advantage of you! You must believe that!"

"Can I see it?" She approached him, and he obligingly spread the fingers of his right hand, showing an ancient ring on the ring finger.

"It's a very good ring." It had the milky luster of white gold, but was turning yellow as white gold does with age. It had an old-fashioned setting with a deep blue, clear sapphire.

"It'd better be . . . Have you considered any of this from my perspective?" Johanna raised her voice. "Imagine how I felt when you disappeared!" She now stood very close to him.

"I have considered it, often," he said. "I'm sorry."

"Oh, you're sorry? My career was nearly ruined!"

Maarten took a deep breath. "Did you ever really love me, Johanna? Or was it just compassion—pity? Did you help me out of pity?"

Johanna scrutinized him. "Do you think I did it out of pity? Do you think I put my job, my reputation, my life, my very identity as a Scholar on the line because of *pity*? Do you think I slept with you out of *pity?* I give homeless people that I pity a few stuivers or doublets, ever since you mentioned the proper rate to me. I certainly don't go around stealing books for them!"

There was an uncomfortable pause. Rain mingled with her tears, but she went on, giving voice to the unspeakable thought that had been clawing at the back of her mind. "I could say the same to you. Did you really love me? Or did you take advantage of me? It's easy to take in a hopeless, naive, middle-aged lady who's aching for some love in her life, isn't it?"

Maarten listened with a rising sense of discomfort. He said, "You shouldn't have done it. You might think you're some sort of savior, but I didn't ask for your help, certainly not for you to take such a risk for me. So you shouldn't complain that I didn't give it right back when it was convenient for you."

Johanna said, "I wasn't expecting gratitude, but I wasn't expecting an ethics lecture either. Okay, theft is wrong, but sometimes you need to go against the law to solve an unjust situation. What I would like to know is why, when you got on your feet and your problems were solved, it never occurred to you to contact me."

"But I left that note! I left you an entire tree, even," Maarten cried, exasperated. "Also, you've got everything so figured out, with your fancy Scholar position and your boat, and stuff, and I was just a nobody, and I felt invisible. I didn't think you would like to see me back."

Johanna said softly, "You were never invisible to me, not even on the first day we met." She added, "The thing is this: I'm forty-seven years old, and I am done settling with being content. I want a chance at happiness, and I believe—and I thought you believed too—that we could be happy. I want to be around you. I love your art, I love talking to you, I want you close to me. Do you feel the same? Or am I just a means to an end to you? Do you want us to give it a try, being happy together? Yes, or no?"

Maarten felt the lump of shame and dread in his throat dissolve. He swallowed hard, and managed to say, "Let's try a shot at happiness."

About the Author

Helen De Cruz is a Philosophy Professor, holder of the Danforth Chair in the Humanities at Saint Louis University. In their spare time, they play the Renaissance lute and archlute. They write fiction, draw and paint. Their fiction has appeared in *EscapePod*, *HyphenPunk*, and *Kaleidotrope*. They are co-editor, with Eric Schwitzgebel and Johan De Smedt, of the anthology *Philosophy Through Science Fiction Stories* (Bloomsbury, 2021). This is their first novella-length work.

About Pink Hydra Press

Founded in 2024 to make a space for new, queer, and weird speculative literature, Pink Hydra Press is the only organization of its kind in Africa. The genre/lit magazine The Pink Hydra has published short stories and poems from dozens of international authors. The book press is just starting out.

If you enjoy stories with a touch of the weird, or if you're an author who loves writing books and poetry infused with weirdness, come visit us at www.thepinkhydra.com.

We publish a variety of genres, but we are particularly interested in queer science fiction and fantasy, stories written by and about women, stories which challenge the current status quo, and spicy romantic and erotic stories.

Many heads. One mission.

MJÖLNIR,
GUNGNIR &
GJALLARHORN
Six heroic tales from the Norse mythology
Retold by
Matias Travieso-Diaz
. . . a must-read for fans of Norse mythology and short stories!
— As reviewed on Amazon.com

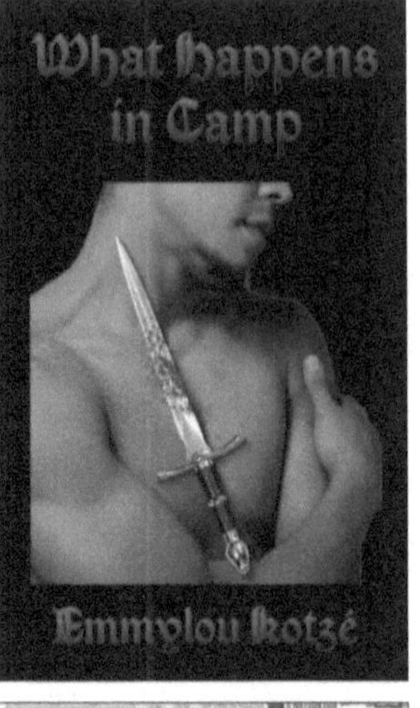
What happens
in Camp
Emmylou kotzé

FOREST OF THE
MORNING
EMMYLOU KOTZÉ

"Maarten and Johanna are characters you will
take into your heart and treasure."
—ERIC KAPLAN, writer and producer,
THE BIG BANG THEORY
HELEN
DE CRUZ
THE ARTISTRY
OF MAGIC

Visit our online stores:

ko-fi.com/thepinkhydra/shop

thepinkhydra.itch.io

. . . or anywhere else where (e)books are sold.

MJÖLNIR, GUNGNIR & GJALLARHORN

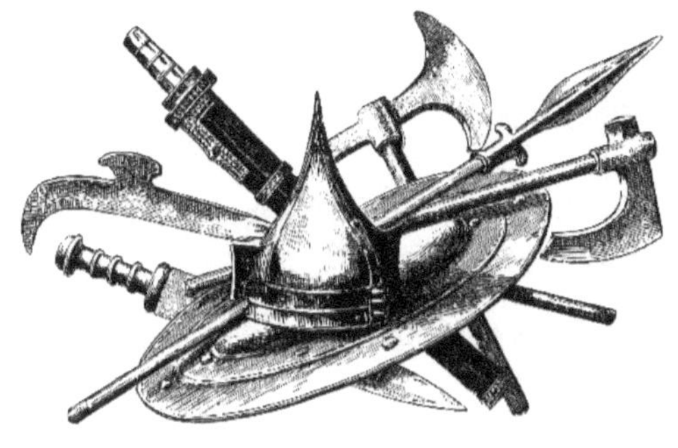

Six heroic tales from the Norse mythology

Retold by Matias Travieso-Diaz

PINK HYDRA PRESS

2024

Copyright